W9-CPA-189

Table of Contents

May

S	M	T	W	T	F	S
	1	2	3	4	(5)	6
7	8	9	10	11	12	13
14	15	16	17	18	19	20
21	22	23	24	25	26	27
28	29	30	31			

4

Cinco de Mayo

by Lola M. Schaefer

Consulting Editor: Gail Saunders-Smith, Ph.D.

Consultant: Gregory S. Rodriguez, Assistant Professor
Mexican American Studies and Research Center
University of Arizona

Pebble Books

an imprint of Capstone Press
Mankato, Minnesota

Pebble Books are published by Capstone Press,
151 Good Counsel Drive, P.O. Box 669, Mankato, Minnesota 56002.
www.capstonepub.com

Copyright © 2002 Capstone Press, a Capstone imprint. All rights reserved.
No part of this publication may be reproduced in whole or in part, or stored in a
retrieval system, or transmitted in any form or by any means, electronic, mechanical,
photocopying, recording, or otherwise, without written permission of the publisher.
For information regarding permission, write to Capstone Press,
151 Good Counsel Drive, P.O. Box 669, Dept. R, Mankato, Minnesota 56002.
Printed in the United States of America in North Mankato, Minnesota.
072011
006231CGVMI

 Books published by Capstone Press are manufactured with paper
containing at least 10 percent post-consumer waste.

Library of Congress Cataloging-in-Publication Data
Schaefer, Lola M., 1950–
    Cinco de Mayo/by Lola M. Schaefer
    p. cm.—(Holidays and celebrations)
    Includes bibliographical references and index.
    Summary: Simple text and photographs explain the history of Cinco de Mayo,
the commemoration of the victory of the Mexican army over the French army on
May 5, 1862, and how it is celebrated.
    ISBN-13: 978-0-7368-0661-9 (hardcover)   ISBN-10: 0-7368-0661-X (hardcover)
    ISBN-13: 978-0-7368-4893-0 (softcover)   ISBN-10: 0-7368-4893-2 (softcover)
    1. Cinco de Mayo (Mexican holiday)—History—Juvenile literature. 2. Cinco de
Mayo, Battle of, 1862—Juvenile literature. 3. Mexico—Social life and customs—
Juvenile literature. [1. Cinco de Mayo (Mexican holiday) 2. Holidays—Mexico.
3. Mexico—Social life and customs.] I. Title. II. Series.
F1233 .S28   2001
394.26972—dc21   00-024165

Note to Parents and Teachers

The Holidays and Celebrations series supports national social studies
standards related to culture. This book describes Cinco de Mayo and
illustrates how it is celebrated. The photographs support early readers in
understanding the text. The repetition of words and phrases helps early
readers learn new words. This book also introduces early readers to subject-
specific vocabulary words, which are defined in the Words to Know
section. Early readers may need assistance to read some words and to use
the Table of Contents, Words to Know, Read More, Internet Sites, and
Index/Word List sections of the book.

Cinco de Mayo is celebrated on May 5. Cinco de Mayo means "fifth of May" in Spanish. Mexican Americans think about their Mexican history on Cinco de Mayo.

Cinco de Mayo is a national holiday in Mexico. People remember the Mexican victory over the French army on this day.

The French army attacked the Mexican city of Puebla on May 5, 1862. The French army was larger than the Mexican army.

The battle lasted only one day. The Mexican army fought hard. They won the Battle of Puebla.

Some people celebrate
Cinco de Mayo with
parades. They ride
on floats and wear
colorful clothes.

14

Some people celebrate
Cinco de Mayo
by dancing.

Some people celebrate
Cinco de Mayo
by singing.

Some people celebrate
Cinco de Mayo
by eating Mexican foods.

Children swing at piñatas
on Cinco de Mayo.
Candy falls when the
piñata breaks.

Words to Know

army—a large group of people trained to fight on land

float—a decorated truck or platform that is part of a parade

Mexican—of or belonging to Mexico

Mexican American—a person who lives in the United States who has Mexican ancestry; Cinco de Mayo celebrations have been popular with Mexican Americans since the 1900s.

national—having to do with a country as a whole

piñata—a hollow, decorated container filled with candy; a person wearing a blindfold tries to break a piñata with a stick.

Spanish—the language that is spoken in Spain, as well as Mexico and other Latin American countries; Spanish is the official language of Mexico.

Read More

MacMillan, Dianne M. *Mexican Independence Day and Cinco de Mayo.* Best Holiday Books. Springfield, N.J.: Enslow, 1997.

Urrutia, María Cristina. *Cinco de Mayo:Yesterday and Today.* Toronto: Groundwood Books, 1999.

Vázquez, Sarah. *Cinco de Mayo.* A World of Holidays. Austin, Texas: Raintree Steck-Vaughn, 1999.

Internet Sites

FactHound offers a safe, fun way to find Internet sites related to this book. All of the sites on FactHound have been researched by our staff.

Here's all you do:

Visit *www.facthound.com*

FactHound will fetch the best sites for you!

Index/Word List

Word Count: 144
Early-Intervention Level: 17

Editorial Credits
Mari C. Schuh, editor; Heather Kindseth, designer; Kimberly Danger and
  Heidi Schoof, photo researchers

Photo Credits
Bob Daemmrich/Pictor, cover
Corbis, 8
Elliot Varner Smith, 12
H. Huntly Hersch, 20
Joe Viesti/The Viesti Collection, 14
Library of Congress, 10
Place Stock Photo, 4, 6, 16
Richard Cummins, 1
Unicorn Stock Photos/Jeff Greenberg, 18

UNIT 10: SCHOOL'S
OUT FOR SUMMER

(LIBRARY)

Holidays and Celebrations

Cinco de Mayo

Cinco de Mayo is celebrated on
May 5. Find out more facts about
Cinco de Mayo inside this book.

Available through
Red Brick Learning
www.redbricklearning.com

Capstone
press®

Capstone Publishers
www.capstonepub.com

CONTAINS AT LEAST 10%
POST-CONSUMER WASTE

ISBN-13: 978-0-7368-4893-0
ISBN-10: 0-7368-4893-2

90000

9 780736 848930